**E**ach Puffin Easy-to-Read book has a color-coded reading level to make book selection easy for parents and children. Because all children are unique in their reading development, Puffin's three levels make it easy for teachers and parents to find the right book to suit each individual child's reading readiness.

**Level 1:**  Short, simple sentences full of word repetition—plus clear visual clues to help children take the first important steps toward reading.

**Level 2:**  More words and longer sentences for children just beginning to read on their own.

**Level 3:**  Lively, fast-paced text—perfect for children who are reading on their own.

*"Readers aren't born, they're made.*
*Desire is planted—planted by*
*parents who work at it."*

**—Jim Trelease**, author of
*The Read-Aloud Handbook*

Emma
Sam
Anna

PUFFIN BOOKS
Published by the Penguin Group
Penguin Books USA Inc., 375 Hudson Street, New York, New York 10014, U.S.A.
Penguin Books Ltd, 27 Wrights Lane, London W8 5TZ, England
Penguin Books Australia Ltd, Ringwood, Victoria, Australia
Penguin Books Canada Ltd, 10 Alcorn Avenue, Toronto, Ontario, Canada M4V 3B2
Penguin Books (N.Z.) Ltd, 182–190 Wairau Road, Auckland 10, New Zealand

Penguin Books Ltd, Registered Offices: Harmondsworth, Middlesex, England

First published in the United States of America by Viking Penguin,
a division of Penguin Books USA Inc., 1991
Simultaneously published in Puffin Books
Published in a Puffin Easy-to-Read edition, 1994

3  5  7  9  10  8  6  4

Text copyright © Fred Ehrlich, 1991
Illustrations copyright © Martha Gradisher, 1991
All rights reserved

Library of Congress Catalog Card Number: 90-53012
ISBN 0-14-036871-X

Puffin® and Easy-to-Read® are registered trademarks of Penguin Books USA Inc.
Printed in the United States of America

Reading Level 2.1

# A VALENTINE FOR MS. VANILLA

Fred Ehrlich
Pictures by Martha Gradisher

PUFFIN BOOKS

It's Valentine's Day.

Ms. Vanilla puts
a Valentine box
on her desk.

"Now, class," she says, "we will make Valentines."

Everybody gets busy.
Very busy.

They all make cards.

They all write poems.

One, two, three, four, five—
the box is stuffed with Valentines.

"Now, class," says Ms. Vanilla,
"it's cleanup time. Clean up.
Then we can have our party."

It's party time in
Ms. Vanilla's class.

Angelina gives out napkins.
Charlene gives out cupcakes.

Donald gives out candy hearts.

And Ms. Vanilla
pours the punch.

"Now, class," says Ms. Vanilla,
"it's time to open Valentines.
Lee Wong, you can pick first."

Lee Wong opens a card.

He reads:

I will cover you with slime
If you won't be my Valentine!

Mary Ann opens a card.
She reads:

I'll be your Valentine, I think,
If you stop telling me I stink.

Donald reads his.

Valentine, you mean more to me
Than watching cartoons on my TV.

Charlene reads hers.

Valentine, I'll stick to you,
Like chewing gum upon my shoe.

Everyone listens to Angelina.

My Valentine is never icky,
Like oatmeal
When it's cold and sticky.

Next comes Paul.

Valentine, you're not so good to eat,
But still I think you're pretty neat.

# Now it's Ben's turn.

I'll climb on Ms. Vanilla's desk,
If my Valentine says
She loves me best.

Melba is last.

Roses are red, violets are blue,
Kiss Ms. Vanilla and I'll kiss you.

Then Rosa says, "Ms. Vanilla, we made a Valentine for you."

For Ms. Vanilla we all cheer,
The greatest teacher of the year.
Here's a heart we all have signed—
Will you be our Valentine?

Angelina Benita
MaryAnn
Max Charlene Ben
Paul
Harry
Rosa Donald